Dragon
Fall Fair

Adapted by Mara Conlon
Based on an original TV episode written by Steven Westren

SCHOLASTIC INC.
New York   Toronto   London   Auckland
Sydney   Mexico City   New Delhi   Hong Kong

ISBN 978-0-545-20054-7

Dragon © 2010 Cité-Amérique – scopas medien AG – Image Plus.
Used under license by Scholastic. All rights reserved.

Published by Scholastic Inc. SCHOLASTIC and associated logos
are trademarks and/or registered trademarks of Scholastic Inc.

12 11 10 9 8 7 6 5 4 3 2 1   10 11 12 13 14/0

Printed in the U.S.A. 40
First printing, July 2010

It was the first day of fall.
"The leaves are red and orange!"
said Dragon.

"It's a good day for a Fall Fair,"
said Beaver.

"What's a Fall Fair?"
asked Dragon.

"A Fall Fair is a party at the start of fall.
There are hayrides and games with apples.
There is even a fun house," Beaver said.

Dragon worked all morning.
He set up his yard for the Fall Fair.

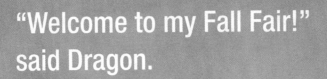

"Welcome to my Fall Fair!"
said Dragon.

"Let's go on a hayride!"
Dragon said.

There was only one problem.
"Giddyup!" said Dragon.

"Surf's up!" said Alligator.

"Hey, hay!" said Ostrich.
The hay would not move!

"You need a horse and cart
to pull the hay," said Beaver.

"What about a dragon with a wagon?"
asked Dragon.

Then it was time to bob for apples.

But Dragon did not have any apples.
So the friends tried to use a pumpkin.

There was only one problem.
The pumpkin was too hard to bite!

But the friends could roll the pumpkins!

Next the friends played in Dragon's fun house. "Look how high I can jump!" said Alligator.

"There is just one last thing!" said Dragon.
"Follow me!"

"Shake your hips and then shout hay!
Sing high ho for the first fall day!"

"I've never been to a Fall Fair like this!" said Beaver.

Dragon giggled and said, "Hooray for fall!"